S0-AWT-160

THIS IS ANT-MAN

Adapted by Chris "Doc" Wyatt

Illustrated by Ron Lim *and* Rachelle Rosenberg

Based on the Marvel comic book series Ant-Man

Los Angeles
New York

marvelkids.com

© 2015 MARVEL

Printed in China
First Box Set Edition, April 2015
9 10
FAC-025393-21151
ISBN 978-1-4847-2178-0
Not for individual resale

This is Scott Lang.

Scott is Ant-Man.
Ant-Man is a Super Hero!

Scott was not always Ant-Man.
He was once a thief.

Scott stole to support his family.

Scott wanted to teach his daughter
right from wrong.
He decided to stop stealing.
He went back to school to study science.

One day, Scott met a scientist named Hank.
They talked about science.

Hank gave Scott a special suit.
Scott tried it on.

Scott shrank to the size of an ant!
It was fun at first.

But then ants chased Scott!

Scott got big again
and saved himself!

Soon Scott found a way
to talk to ants.

Then they were his friends.

Scott became Ant-Man.

Ant-Man fights Super Villains.

Ant-Man uses the ants as an army.

Now Ant-Man helps the Avengers.

Being small helps Ant-Man
do special things.

Bad guys cannot see him coming.

Ant-Man can fit in small places.

Ant-Man can surprise bad guys!

Ant-Man likes working with Iron Man.

Ant-Man and Iron Man
make a good team.

Ant-Man is very strong!

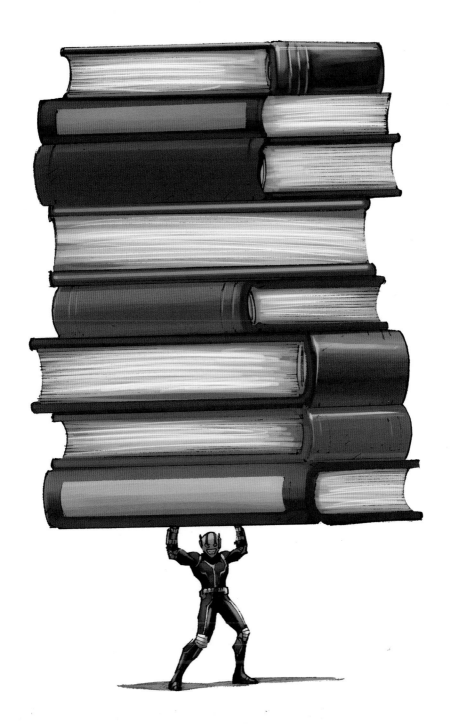

Ant-Man can turn from big to tiny.

Ant-Man fights for good.

Ant-Man has lots of
Super Hero friends.

They help each other
fight the bad guys!

Ant-Man is a true hero.